G- 13

ENID BLYTON'S

STORIES FOR YOU

Enid Blyton's

STORIES FOR YOU

PRINTED IN   GREAT BRITAIN
DEAN & SON Ltd.
41/43 Ludgate Hill   LONDON EC4

Made and Printed in Great Britain by Purnell & Sons, Ltd.
Paulton (Somerset) and London

CONTENTS

The Quiet Little Boy

"COME and play football!" yelled John to Barry. "Come on!"

"No thanks," said Barry. "I'm going fishing."

"Fishing! When you could play football!" said John, and stalked off in disgust.

"Come and play pirates!" shouted Tom, as he came up behind Barry. "We want somebody else. It's a most exciting game."

"No. I'm busy, I'm going fishing," said Barry.

"Pooh! Playing pirates is much more exciting!" said Tom. "My mother says you're too quiet. She says you ought to play rough games."

"Why?" asked Barry. "*I* don't say you're too noisy, you ought to do something peaceful! Everyone isn't the same. My father is a fisherman, my grandfather is, too. We all like sitting by a river, waiting for a fish to bite, and watching all the birds and animals around."

And then Jack came up and slapped Barry on the shoulder. "Are you going to the river? So are we—but we're going to row and to bathe. You come too."

"No thanks. I'm going fishing," said Barry once more. "I don't keep bothering you to come and fish—so don't keep bothering me to do things I don't want to do."

"There goes the quiet little boy," shouted Jack, as Barry went off. "The good and quiet little boy!"

"He wouldn't climb a tree, he'd be afraid to go out in a boat, he'd hate a game of football!" cried Tom. This wasn't true, but he was being unkind. He was a noisy, rough boy himself, and he didn't like to see somebody quiet. He

couldn't imagine why a boy should like fishing and watching birds and insects and animals.

Barry went down the lane to the river, feeling hurt. He never worried the others to come and fish with *him*! Why should they laugh and jeer at him because he wouldn't always go with them and do the things *they* liked? Playing football and rowing a boat were no better things than fishing. They are all nice things to do.

He found a peaceful spot and sat down in the grass. He had brought his lunch with him, and

9

a book if he wanted to read. He looked at his fine new rod in delight.

"You're a beauty," he said, as he fitted it together. "A real beauty. You'll catch me some fine fish for supper. Now let's hope the shining kingfisher will come along today and do a bit of fishing too. And perhaps the water-vole will come and have a look at me as he did the other day."

He settled down, his rod over the river, the

line running down into the water. His float bobbed on the surface, and Barry watched it. When it bobbed below the water he knew he had caught a fish that was pulling hard, and making the little red float jerk up and down.

But no fish came yet. Still, the kingfisher came instead! He sat on a low branch, shining green and blue, his long, strong beak ready to catch a fish. "Ah—there was one." The brilliant bird dived straight into the water and came back with a small fish in its beak. It tossed it into the air and swallowed it.

"Very clever," said Barry, softly. "But don't take *all* the fish, will you? Leave a few for me."

It was lovely sitting there in the sunshine, watching the kingfisher, and looking out for the moor-hen and her young ones bobbing along. A hedgehog suddenly came by and a grey squirrel hopped down. Barry was very happy.

And then Jack came up with the others and spoilt it all!

"Ah—here's the quiet little boy again, in a quiet little place, doing a quiet bit of fishing!" he said. "Let's throw some stones into the water and frighten the fish away."

"Don't be silly," said Barry. But Jack was already throwing stones and earth into the water, and so did the others. And then George threw Barry's lunch into the water, too!

"That's a beastly thing to do," said Barry, angrily. "You know I can't go home and get some more, it's so far to walk. You ought to be ashamed of yourself, George."

"Have a fight?" said George, dancing round with his fists up. "You don't dare to! You wouldn't dare to do anything brave or plucky! Quiet little boy!"

"Shut up, George! You've done enough by

throwing Barry's lunch away," said Jack, who felt sorry about that. "Come on. Let's go for a row."

They went off, leaving Barry hurt and angry. His nice lunch floating out there on the water! It was too bad. He felt as if he hated rough, rude George.

He heard the boys go up the river to get the boat that they sometimes borrowed. He heard the sound of oars. Then the boat came into view, with Jack and George pulling at an oar each. Pat was steering. The others were pummelling each other in the bottom of the boat.

And then, quite suddenly, something happened! The boys punching each other made the boat sway violently. Jack gave one of them a kick, and the boy sat up angrily.

"Did you kick me, Jack? You stop it!"

And he fell on Jack and began to pummel him. The oar slipped from Jack's hand and went floating down the river. Jack clutched the side of the boat, shouting at the angry boy.

"Stop it, Fred, stop it, I say! You'll have the boat over!"

And just as he said that the boat rocked so violently that it turned right over! Into the water went all the boys, with screams and splashes!

The other oar went floating off too. The boat drifted towards the opposite bank. The boys began to swim towards Barry.

Jack reached the bank first. Then Fred, then Leslie. Pat came next, quite out of breath, and behind him, hardly able to reach the bank, was Sam.

"Where's George?" said Jack. Fred stood shivering on the bank and pointed.

"There! He's a poor swimmer, you know. Hey, George, come on, idiot! Here's the bank. Come on. Strike out."

But George was terrified. He was in such a panic that he hardly remembered how to swim. He sank down under the water and then came up, gasping and spluttering and choking.

"Help!" he cried, feebly. "Help!"

"I say—he won't drown, will he?" said Jack, alarmed. "GEORGE! Strike out!"

"Hadn't one of us better go in and help him?" asked Fred.

"He'd only pull us under," said Pat. "Come ON, George."

But George couldn't reach the bank. Jack waded in and held out his hand, but George was too far away. They threw one end of a piece of rope to him, which he managed to hold on to, but it broke as they dragged him near to the bank. Poor George went under for the second time. What could they do?

And then Barry ran up to them with his long fishing-rod. "Get out of the way!" he shouted to Jack. "I'll reach him with my new rod—it'll just about reach."

The boys watched, breathlessly. Barry held
out the rod. It touched George as he came to
the surface, and the boy grasped it desperately.
"Hang on. We'll pull you in," cried Fred, and
he and Barry pulled hard at the rod, drawing
George towards the bank. Jack helped him to
climb up and he fell on the grass, choking and
sobbing.

"It's all right, George," said Barry. "You're
safe. You'd better all race home before you get
chills."

"Your rod's broken," said Jack suddenly. "I'm sorry about that, Barry. You saved George's life—and your new rod gets broken. You've—you've been awfully decent."

"Go on home," said Barry. "You're shivering."

The boys went home, taking poor, frightened George with them. Barry went home, too, sad about his broken rod. He didn't tell anyone how it had got broken.

But that night George's father came round to Barry's house and asked to see Barry. As soon as he came into the room the man shook hands with him and clapped him on the back. "You're a hero! You saved George's life, and I can't thank you enough. What did your father and mother say about it?"

"We don't know anything about it!" said Barry's mother, astonished. "What did Barry do?" So she was told.

George's father shook Barry by the hand again. "You're a quiet little fellow, Barry, and not very big—but my word you're worth ten of the others. Look out for a visit from the boys next week!"

And will you believe it, on the following Wednesday up came all the boys, headed by George, who carried a magnificent new fishing-rod!

On it was a label—"For the quiet little boy, with cheers from:

the Noisy Ones."

And the queer thing is that one of them always goes fishing with Barry now. Guess who? Yes—George!

The Very Fierce Carpenter

MR. CHIP the carpenter had a very exciting workshop. He was always making or mending all kinds of things and the boys loved to go and look at his tools. He had so many—hammers, saws, screwdrivers, chisels—and it was marvellous to watch the way he used them.

But Mr. Chip didn't like the boys. "Little pests!" he called them. "Miserable little mischiefs! Rude little monkeys!"

So, of course, although the boys liked Mr. Chip's shop they didn't like *him*. They made up a very silly game just to tease him. The game was to dart into his shop and pick up some shavings from the floor before he could stop them. At the end of the week the boys each counted their shavings and the one who had the most was their leader for the next week.

"It's a very silly game," said Jack's mother, when she heard of it. "And it will only make Mr. Chip angry."

"But the shavings aren't worth anything to him, and it's fun to see who can get the most," said Jack. "He shouldn't be so cross and grumpy, Mother. He doesn't even like us to watch him when he's making something—and he's really very clever."

This silly game really made Mr. Chip very cross indeed—so cross that one day he bought a dog! It was only a puppy at first, but it would soon grow. "And I'll teach him to fly at any boy who dares to come into my shop!" said Mr. Chip, hammering away.

The boys would have liked the puppy—and the puppy would have liked the boys—but Mr. Chip taught it to bark and fly at any boy who dared to dart into his shop to pick up a shaving. Soon the puppy could growl and show its teeth.

"One of these days that puppy will be a big dog, and will bite one of you," Jack's mother said. "It's too bad of Mr. Chip to make it so fierce—I do so wish you boys would stop teasing the carpenter. You make *him* fierce, too, and he's not really a bad fellow at all."

The puppy grew and grew. It adored Mr. Chip, and Mr. Chip thought it was the best dog in the world. He and the dog were always together, except when Mr. Chip sent it for his paper in the afternoon.

"Now, Wags—off you go for my paper," he would say. And Wags would run out of the shop to the paper man at the corner, and bring back a paper in his mouth. The boys thought that was very clever of him. They were afraid of Wags now. He seemed as fierce as his master! It had got quite dangerous to dart into the shop and pick up a shaving. Peter nearly got bitten!

"Horrible dog—and horrible master!" said Kenneth. "I've a good mind to throw a stone at Wags when he goes to fetch the afternoon paper for Mr. Chip."

"No, don't," said Jack. "That would be a hateful thing to do."

The boys found that the only safe time to dart into the shop and snatch up shavings from the floor was when Wags was out fetching the afternoon paper! But Mr. Chip was ready for them! He caught Kenneth by his collar and shook him till the boy was afraid his teeth would fall out.

He caught Ned and rubbed his nose in a pile of sawdust. He nearly caught Jack, and bellowed so loudly at him that Jack dropped the shavings he had snatched up!

"Little pest! Wait till I get you!" he roared. "I'll set my dog on you!"

Now Jack had a very big wooden engine,

23

painted red. It wasn't big enough for him to get into the cab, which was a pity—but it was quite big enough to take when he went shopping for his mother, because it could carry all the things he bought! He used to stuff them into the cab of his big red engine, and then take them home like that.

The other boys thought it was a grand engine. "Be grander still if it had trucks," said Kenneth. "We could all go shopping together

then for our mothers, and use a truck each for our parcels. That would make shopping fun."

"Well, there's only room for *my* shopping," said Jack, afraid that the boys might want to use his engine for all their parcels, too. It would be very heavy to pull then! "This kind of wooden engine doesn't have trucks."

The mothers all smiled to see Jack go shopping, pulling his big engine along empty first of all—and then going back with the cab piled high with all kinds of things. It was wonderful what that engine carried! It even managed to bring home half a sack of potatoes once.

One afternoon Jack's mother called to him, "Jack! Where are you? Oh, you're there, reading. I'm so sorry, dear, but I quite forgot to ask you to take your blazer to be cleaned when you went shopping this morning. It won't be back in time for the beginning of term if you don't take it today. Will you take it now for me?"

"Right, Mother," said Jack, cheerfully. He really was a very good-tempered boy. He got up and went to fetch his engine.

"Oh, don't bother to take your engine, just to carry your *blazer*!" said his mother. "Surely you can take it over your arm, Jack!"

"My engine likes a run," said Jack. "It's like a dog—it loves a walk!"

He pulled the big engine from its place in the hall cupboard, and stuffed the blazer into the cab. Then he hauled on the rope. "Come on," he said. "We'll hurry there and back, then I can get on with my book."

But something happened on the way there.

Mr. Chip had sent his dog Wags out for his afternoon paper at just the same time as Jack was taking his blazer to the cleaner's. Wags had gone to the man at the corner, dropped a penny out of his mouth on to the pavement, and let the paper man stuff a folded paper between his teeth.

He turned to go back to Mr. Chip, when a much bigger dog growled at him. Wags growled back. The dog flew at Wags, and Wags leapt sideways into the road.

There was a loud squeak of brakes, and a car

27

swerved suddenly. But it didn't stop soon enough. It hit poor Wags on the back legs, and the dog crumpled up on the road with a howl. The paper fell from his mouth.

Jack was just nearby with his big engine. He saw it all happen. The big dog ran off at once. The car-driver got out of his car, and two or three children ran up. Wags tried to get up but he couldn't. His back legs were hurt.

"Who does this dog belong to? Does anyone know?" asked the car-driver.

"Yes. It belongs to Mr. Chip, the carpenter," said Jack, coming up with his engine. "Oh, poor Wags! He's hurt! He can't get up."

"I'll go along in the car and tell Mr. Chip to come and fetch his dog," said the driver, and he got into the car again. He drove off. But alas, he didn't go to Mr. Chip's. He drove straight past, and went on his way.

Jack waited and waited for Mr. Chip to come, but he didn't. Wags dragged himself painfully to the pavement, picking up his master's paper in his mouth. Jack was very, very sorry for him.

"Wags! *I'll* take you to Mr. Chip," said the boy at last. "That car-driver can't have told him. But how can I take you?"

Wags whined mournfully. Then Jack had a wonderful idea. He would pick Wags up gently and put him on his blazer in the cab of the engine! Then he would pull the dog all the way to Mr. Chip's shop.

"You won't be shaken too much because you'll be on my blazer," he told Wags. "I'm

going to pick you up. I'll try not to hurt you.
Don't bite me, will you, because I'm only trying
to help you?"

Luckily Wags wouldn't let go the paper he
held in his mouth, so although he growled a
little with pain when Jack gently lifted him, he
couldn't snap or bite.

Jack laid him on the blazer. "Now you'll be
all right," he said. "Soon be home, Wags!"

He dragged the engine slowly down the

road, trying not to shake the hurt dog. Children followed him, and Wags growled again because he had been taught not to like boys and girls.

Soon Jack was at Mr. Chip's shop. He left the engine outside and went in. Mr. Chip was sawing and didn't see Jack at first. But when he caught sight of the boy out of the corner of his eye he pounced on him at once.

"Ah! Got you this time!" he shouted.

"Mr. Chip! Don't shake me! MR. CHIP! WAGS HAS BEEN HURT!" yelled Jack.

Mr. Chip stopped shaking him. "What's that? Wags hurt? Where is he?"

"He got knocked down by a car," said Jack. "I was there. He can't walk with his back legs. So I put him in the cab of my big wooden engine on my old blazer, and brought him along. He's just outside. I couldn't bring the engine up the steps."

In a trice Mr. Chip was outside. In a trice he had Wags in his arms, and the dog dropped the newspaper and licked his master feebly. "I'm going to the vet!" said Mr. Chip to Jack. "Keep the shop for me while I'm gone. My poor dog! He's badly hurt!"

Well! There was Jack left in charge of the carpenter's shop! What an extraordinary thing! He looked all round it. He felt the big heavy hammers. He admired the little stool the carpenter was making. He wished he could try out the big plane and the saw. What a lovely shop to have!

His friends came peeping in at him, amazed to see him there alone. He told them what had happened.

"Ooooh! We could take every single

shaving off the floor while Mr. Chip's gone,"
said Kenneth, at once.

"No. I'm in charge," said Jack. "That
would be a silly thing to do. Anyway, he's
dreadfully upset about Wags. We couldn't do
silly or mean things when he's upset."

"Serves him right," said Ned. "I'm glad that
bad-tempered dog is hurt."

"Oh, no. You'd have been sorry if you'd
seen him," said Jack. "Leave those nails

33

alone, Kenneth. You're not to take a single one."

"I wasn't going to," said Kenneth. "I was just running them through my fingers. They feel nice."

"Here's Mr. Chip," said Ned, suddenly, and all the boys ran away at once. Only Jack was left, standing in the shop. Mr. Chip came in. He hadn't got Wags with him.

"Where's Wags?" asked Jack, at once.

"I've left him at the vet's," said Mr. Chip. "Got to have something done to his leg, poor fellow."

Jack was shocked to see tears in the carpenter's eyes. He must love Wags very, very much.

"Will he be all right?" asked Jack.

"Perhaps," said Mr. Chip. "Don't know yet. I shall miss him badly. Thanks for bringing him back to me in that engine of yours."

Jack went home. He forgot about taking his blazer to the cleaner's, but when he told his mother what had happened she quite understood. People can't think of dirty blazers when dogs are hurt.

34

Every day Jack went to Mr. Chip's shop and asked the same question. "Any news of Wags?"

And Mr. Chip would tell him the latest news. "Not so good." Or perhaps, "He's better today." And then, "He may be back next week."

Once Mr. Chip asked Jack to bring back his afternoon paper for him. Jack stuck it into the cab of his engine with his other shopping. Mr. Chip stared at the big engine and said what a fine thing it was to bring back shopping in. Jack agreed. He was still rather scared of Mr. Chip, but he rather liked talking to him and watching him at work. Mr. Chip didn't chase him away now.

"Wags is coming home tomorrow!" said Mr. Chip at last. He was smiling all over his rather fierce face. "You might come in and see him. He can walk all right but he limps a bit still. Can you come? He's got something for you."

Jack did go the next day, of course. Wags was there, looking rather thin, and limping quite a bit—but how his tail wagged when he saw Jack. He barked and then licked the boy all over his knees and hands and face.

"Good to have him back again," said Mr. Chip. "Now you come and see what he's got for you, Jack. Just a little present for some-one who did him and me a good turn. A good turn to someone who's always yelled at you, and a good turn to a dog that's been taught to bark at you and chase you off! That's something worth doing."

He took Jack into his little sitting-room

behind the shop. Jack stared in astonishment and delight—for there, beautifully made, were three fine trucks, one painted red, one blue and one yellow!

"Trucks for that fine engine of yours that pulled my Wags home that day," said Mr. Chip. "A present from Wags himself!"

"Oh, Mr. *Chip*!" said Jack, and he flung his arms round Wags and hugged him. "Thank you, Wags, thank you. And thank *you*, Mr. Chip. You made them for me. They're marvellous. Now all the children in my street can go shopping with me and my engine can bring all the shopping home in its new trucks. I say! What *will* the boys say! You won't mind them using the trucks you've made, will you?"

"Not a bit," said Mr. Chip, delighted to see Jack's excitement. "Come in any time you like, any of you, and watch me at work. Be glad to see you, and so will Wags."

You should have seen Jack going home with his engine and three gay trucks behind! All the boys came out to watch—what a wonderful sight! "Present from Wags and Mr. Chip," said Jack, proudly. "And Mr. Chip says we can go in his shop any time we like. What do you think of *that*?"

And now Mr. Chip often has his shop full of boys, and he doesn't mind a bit. As for Wags, he's as happy as can be to have so many new friends. He still limps, so you'll know him if you see him, by his limp and his crooked left hind leg. Give him a pat for me if you meet him!

The Bit of Barley-Sugar

ONCE when Simon bit a stick of barley-sugar, a piece of it broke right off and fell on the floor.

Simon knelt down to look for it. "If you find the bit you've dropped, you must go and wash it before you eat it," said his mother. "It may be dirty."

But Simon couldn't find it, though he looked everywhere. He soon gave it up and didn't bother about it any more.

But one of the toys had seen where it went! The wooden bear belonging to the Noah's ark

had seen it roll right over the carpet and go down a little mouse-hole in the wall. He stared and stared at the hole.

"Tonight I'll go and look in the hole and see if I can get out the barley-sugar," he thought. "I shan't tell anyone at all. It shall be my barley-sugar!"

So that night when he thought no one was looking he went to the mouse-hole.

He knelt down by the hole and put in his head. The barley-sugar was *just* inside! The bear was pleased. But he didn't want to get it out in case the others saw him and came to share it. So he stood with his head inside the

hole and licked the barley-sugar. It was lovely and sweet.

The bear licked until he had had enough. He thought he would back out and go and play. He would go and have another lick when he felt like it. He wouldn't tell anyone at all about that lovely barley-sugar!

He backed out and looked round. The clockwork mouse was nearby, looking at him in great astonishment. "Why did you stand so long with your head in the hole?" he asked the wooden bear. "You looked funny."

"Mind your own business," said the bear, rudely, and went away. The clockwork mouse

41

stood and thought for a minute and then he went to the hole. He stuck his head inside, too—and dear me, what was that nice sweet smell?

"Barley-sugar! A bit of barley-sugar! And that bear's been licking it all by himself, the greedy thing!" thought the mouse. "I'll pull it out."

But he couldn't. So he, too, stood and licked and licked till he felt sick. Then he backed out quickly, hoping the bear hadn't seen him. He backed straight into one of the toy soldiers.

"Look out!" said the toy soldier, almost falling over. "Do tell me, clockwork mouse— why have you stood so still with your nose in the mouse-hole for such a very long time? You looked most peculiar!"

"Mind your own business," said the clock-work mouse, just as rudely as the bear, and ran away. The toy soldier was puzzled. Was there someone down the hole to talk to?

He went and stuck his head inside—and he saw the barley-sugar at once! He tried to get right into the hole to get it, but he couldn't

because his toy gun stuck fast. So he just put his head in as far as he could go, and licked. He licked and licked.

"Delicious!" he said. "But I can't lick any more. My tongue is very tired."

He backed out of the hole and saw one of the little dolls' house dolls watching him in surprise.

"What are you doing down that hole?" she said. "You did look funny."

"Mind your own business!" said the toy soldier, very rudely indeed, and he pointed his gun at her. She squealed and hid behind the brick-box. As soon as the toy soldier had gone she ran up to the mouse-hole and peeped down.

"A bit of barley-sugar! Oh! So *that's* what he keeps down there!" said the dolls' house doll. "Well, *I'll* have it all for myself."

But she couldn't get it out—so she, too, had to put in her head and lick. Lickity-lick! How nice and sweet it was. She was sorry when she couldn't lick any more.

She backed out—and dear me, there was a big skittle watching her in astonishment. "What are you doing? What's down there?" he said.

"Mind your own business!" said the doll,
rudely, and went to wash her sticky face.

The skittle poked his wooden head down.
What! Barley-sugar! He poked at it with his
head—and, alas, he poked it so far down the
hole that he couldn't even lick it. He was very
sad indeed. He came out, and went to tell the
other skittles.

While he was gone the Noah's Ark bear
came up. He thought he would have another
little lick, so he stuck his head inside the hole.
But what had happened? He simply couldn't

reach the barley-sugar! It was much too far down—and will you believe it, when he tried to wriggle after it, he got stuck so fast that he couldn't get out of the hole.

He roared and wriggled—and a little live mouse came running up the hole in surprise. She bumped into the barley-sugar. "Oh! Are you shouting to tell me you've pushed a bit of barley-sugar down my hole for me to eat?" she cried. "Thank you very very much, bear!" And she picked it up in her mouth and ran off with it down her hole to her nest.

The farmer from the toy farm pulled the bear out of the hole. The bear was very angry. "The mouse took my bit of barley-sugar. He took it!"

"It wasn't yours, it was mine," said the clockwork mouse.

"Ooooh, fibber! It was *mine*!" said the toy soldier.

"No, no—it belonged to *me*!" said the dolls' house doll.

"It *should* have been mine," said the skittle, sadly. "But I poked it too far down the hole!"

"Oh—so it was *you* who did that!" roared the

angry bear, and he flew at the skittle and knocked him over. Mr. Noah came up from the Noah's Ark, very cross to see such behaviour.

"Stop that now," he said. "Bear, clockwork mouse, soldier, dolls' house doll, and skittle, go into the ark at once. Greediness must be punished. I'm ashamed of you all!"

And will you believe it, he shut them all up in his Ark the whole night long, and they were very sad indeed, left by themselves in the dark. As for the barley-sugar, the mouse's children have a lick at it for a reward whenever they are good. It won't last much longer. It's almost gone!

THE STORM

Hark! The thunder roars aloud
Black is every lowering cloud,
Swift the lightning comes and goes,
All around the storm-wind blows.
Now there comes the falling rain.
Crash! The thunder speaks again.
What a grand and lovely sight
Is a storm by day or night!

Funny Little Mankie

MANKIE was a funny little cat without a tail. She was a Manx cat, which was why she was called Mankie. She had just a stump where her tail should be, as all Manx cats have.

At first, when she was only a kitten, she kept in the house and garden. She was afraid to go very far. She was even afraid of the dead leaves that bounded about in the wind!

She didn't know any other animals at all. Sometimes she put her head round the playroom door and looked at the toys there—but when the ball bounced over to her, she was frightened and fled away.

Then, when she grew bigger, she got bolder —and one night, when she put her head round the playroom door, the toys called to her.

"Come along in. Who are you? What's your name?"

"I'm Mankie," said the little cat, and came right in.

"She's a mankie," said the toys to one another. "What's a mankie?"

48

Nobody knew. "Well—I'm a *monkey*, but she's nothing like *me*," said the toy monkey. "My tail is much, much longer than the mankie's."

"How long is your tail?" the golliwog asked Mankie. "Turn round with your back to us and let us see. If you've got a long tail you can swing by, you may be a kind of monkey, not a mankie."

Mankie turned and the toys all exclaimed loudly: "Why, you haven't *got* a tail!"

"Where's your tail?"

"Have you lost it?"

Mankie was astonished. She had never even *thought* about tails before. She looked at Monkey's beautiful long one. She looked at the toy dog's short one, and the toy horse's long hairy one. Then she looked at herself.

"My tail certainly isn't there," she said, sadly. "I must have dropped it somewhere."

The toys thought that was quite likely.

"The horse lost *his* tail once," said the golliwog. "It came unstuck and dropped out. He didn't notice it for a long time, and he spent all night long looking for it."

"Hrrrumph," said the big rocking-horse, suddenly, making everyone jump. "*My* tail went, too, once. A naughty boy pulled it right out. My word, I did feel cold without it!"

"Do you feel cold behind, little mankie?" said the golliwog.

"Perhaps I do, a bit," said Mankie. "Oh, dear—goodness *knows* where I've dropped my tail. It might be *any*where in the house!"

"If this mankie had a tail, she would be rather like a cat," said the toy horse. "Let's all go and look for her tail."

So they all slipped out of the playroom and went down the stairs to hunt for Mankie's tail. Mankie went too.

"What's your tail like?" asked the golliwog. "Is it black or white, or what?"

Mankie thought hard. "I don't know," she said at last. "I've never noticed."

"Did you ever swing yourself upside down by it, like this?" said the toy monkey, and suddenly leapt up to the banister and hung himself upside down by his tail. Mankie stared in surprise.

"Oh no. I'm sure I never hung myself up by

my tail," she said. "I would have noticed that, I'm sure." They met a little mouse down in the hall. He ran into his hole, and then peeped out, only his little black nose showing.

"Mouse! Have you found a tail lying about anywhere?" asked the toy monkey.

"No. Indeed I haven't," said the mouse. "Why, who has lost one?"

"This animal here—a mankie," said the monkey. The mouse stared at Mankie and got further down his hole. "Looks like a cat to me, not a mankie," he said in fright. "Anyway, it's not having *my* tail!" And away down his

hole he went, his long thin tail behind him.

"Silly mouse," said the golliwog. "As if anyone wants *his* skinny tail! Come on—we'll go to the kitchen and see if the window's open. If it is we'll go and ask the dog if he's seen your tail anywhere."

The dog was next door's dog. Mankie had heard him bark but she hadn't seen him. She was afraid of this big creature in his kennel. The toys pushed her forward.

"Rover! Have you seen a mankie-tail about

anywhere?" asked the toy dog. "This creature here, a mankie, has lost one!"

Rover stared at Mankie, who began to shiver in fright. "Dear me—do you feel cold because you've lost your tail?" asked Rover. "Was it a big one that you could wrap yourself up in, like a squirrel's?"

"No, I don't think so," said Mankie. "I don't *remember* wrapping myself up in it. It couldn't have been a very *big* tail."

"Let's make sure it's gone," said Rover, and he laughed when Mankie turned her back on him. "Good gracious! You've just a stump, that's all. Are you sure nobody's bitten it off?"

"I'm quite sure of *that*!" said Mankie. "I'd have felt somebody biting it off."

"Was it a tail anything like mine?" asked Rover, and he suddenly came right out of his kennel and stood with his back to Mankie. He wagged his big tail so fast that he knocked both the monkey and the golliwog right over!

"Good gracious!" said Mankie, in astonishment. "What a wonderful tail! I'd like one like that!"

"Yes. It's got a very, very good wag in it, hasn't it?" said Rover, pleased. "You can't get tails like that in a hurry!"

"Well, I wouldn't mind a smaller one if it had a good wag," said Mankie. "Where can I get one? I know I shall never, never find mine."

Rover lay down in his kennel and thought. "You might go to the little imp who lives in the cucumber frame," he said. "There aren't any cucumbers there now, because it's winter-time, so you'll easily find him. His name's

56

Snorty. He knows a wonderful lot of magic."

"Yes. His mother was the servant of a wizard," said the golliwog. "He told me. Snorty *might* be able to grow a new tail for the mankie."

So they all went off to find Snorty. He was certainly in the cucumber frame because they could hear him snoring!

"His name should be Snorey not Snorty," said the golliwog, with a giggle, and he rapped on the glass of the frame.

Snorty woke up and squeezed out of a

broken pane of glass. He looked in surprise at the toys. "Hallo," he said. "What's all this, in the middle of the night?"

"We've come to ask you if you can grow a new tail on this mankie," replied the golliwog. "She's lost hers, and we can't find it anywhere."

Snorty looked at Mankie, and gave a little snort. "What a peculiar creature—a bit like a cat. What sort of a tail did she have?"

"She doesn't know," said the monkey.

"Then I can't grow her a new tail," said Snorty.

"Well, I'll have a tail like Rover's, with a wag in it," said Mankie.

"Oh, no you won't," said Snorty, with a bigger snort. "That would take up almost all the magic I've got. Anyway, what's the use of a big wag to you? You'd fall over every time you wagged your tail!"

"I wouldn't," said Mankie, crossly.

"Now, don't squabble," said the toy horse. "What about a smaller tail, Snorty!"

"I tell you, I can't grow the mankie a tail unless I know exactly what a mankie-tail is *like*," said Snorty. "That's my last word." He

began to climb back into the cucumber frame, but the golliwog caught hold of his collar.

"No. Wait a minute," he said. "If you can't grow a new tail, you can surely get back her old one for her! You know enough magic for that."

"All right, all right," said Snorty. "I've a Come-Back spell somewhere. I'll give it to the mankie. If she swallows it, her tail will come slithering up to her out of the darkness, and she'll have it again!"

He felt in his pockets and brought out a little yellow pill that shone strangely in the moonlight. "Here you are," he said to Mankie. "It's got a Come-Back spell in it. Swallow it, think hard of Tails, and your own will come back to you, no matter where you left it."

Mankie swallowed the strange, yellow pill. Everyone waited for the tail to come back, but it didn't. Once the golliwog gave a shout because he thought it was coming, but it was only a worm on the grass.

After they had waited for five minutes, they called out to Snorty, who had gone back to his home in the cucumber frame. "Hey, Snorty! The tail hasn't come back. Your spell's no good."

Snorty was very angry. He threw showers of earth out of the hole in the glass over everyone. "How dare you say my spell is no good! It's a very powerful one. Go away, you ungrateful creatures!"

Very sadly they all went back home. On the way they met the big black cat from next door. He stared in surprise.

"It's all right. It's only us," said the monkey.

"We got a Come-Back spell from Snorty to get back this mankie's tail—but the spell was a failure. The tail didn't come back."

"Snorty's spells are never failures," said the black cat. "The mankie couldn't have had a tail. Who ever heard of a mankie *or* its tail! Where's this queer creature?"

The moon sailed out from behind a cloud. The toys pushed Mankie forward. "Look— this is the mankie, who lost her tail."

The big black cat looked and looked. Then

c   61

he laughed with a loud yowl that frightened all the toys.

"He-hee-hee-ow-hee-ow! That's not a mankie—it's a *cat*. A Manx cat without a tail! Manx cats never do have tails, didn't you know that? No wonder the Come-Back spell was no good. A mankie indeed—she's just a cat like me! I knew her mother and *she* hadn't a tail either! He-hee-hee-ow!"

Well, well, well! Mankie and the toys were most astonished. The golliwog was cross with Mankie. "You told us you were a mankie and had lost your tail," he said. "And you're not. You're just an ordinary cat that hasn't got one."

"I said my *name* was Mankie!" wept poor Mankie. "I didn't say I was a mankie—and it was *you* who told me I'd lost my tail! Oh, dear, oh, dear—now I'll never, never have one!"

And poor Mankie rushed indoors and curled up in her basket, very miserable indeed. But when she heard next day that Rover had chased the big black cat and nipped the top off his tail, she couldn't help feeling that after all it was a very, very good thing that she hadn't got one! She went to tell the toys this and they agreed, too. The monkey asked the golliwog to tie his tail safely round his middle, just in *case* he met Rover that day.

"I'm *glad* I haven't a tail," said Mankie. "It might be such a nuisance. I'd have to be sure I didn't lose the wag out of it. I'd have to see that Rover didn't bite it. And if I swung upside down on it like Monkey does, I might fall and bump my head. I'm very, very glad I *haven't* got a tail!"

Have you ever seen a Manx cat? They're just like Mankie, without a tail at all!

Mr. Squiggle

"CATHY, *will* you stop scribbling over everything?" said Mummy. "Look here—you've made squiggles and scribbles on the kitchen wall—and I've found some silly squiggles on the door of the shed outside. Why do you do it?"

"Well, I can't write words properly yet," said Cathy, "and I'm not very good at drawing. So I just do squiggles—like this!"

And will you believe it, she took her pencil and did a squiggle on the nice, clean tablecloth!

Mummy took her pencil away from her. "Very well—if you are as silly as all that, you shan't have a pencil!" she said.

But Cathy had got such a habit of scribbling here, there and everywhere that she simply couldn't do without something in her fingers for scribbling. She found a blue crayon and began scribbling on the doorstep with it.

So Mummy took that away, too. Then Cathy found a piece of white blackboard chalk, and dear me, the mess she made with that!

There were squiggles on the garden gate and scribbles on the garden seat!

Even Daddy got angry. "Each time I find a squiggle, I shall smack your fingers," he said. "If *you* can't stop them scribbling, I will!"

"I do hope she won't grow up into one of those dreadful people who sign their names everywhere," said Mummy. "I can't think why she does it—she doesn't even write words—it's just squiggles!"

Cathy didn't stop squiggling and scribbling. She got into trouble for it at school, too,

because she scribbled all over the wall next to her seat in class.

"One of these days," said Miss Brown, the teacher, to Cathy, "you'll meet Mr. Squiggle, who knows the language of squiggles—and, dear me, won't you be surprised at the nonsense you've written! *You* can't understand it, but he'll be able to!"

Cathy was certain that Miss Brown was joking, and she laughed. But will you believe it, the very next day she did meet Mr. Squiggle!

She was going home from school. She had with her a piece of red chalk, and she was simply longing to scribble on something with it. When she came to one of the sheds belonging to Mr. Straw, the farmer, she began to scribble all over it in red. It really looked horrid, and quite spoilt the shed.

And then she heard a squeaky voice behind her. "How *dare* you sign my name like that! I *wondered* who it was writing my name everywhere—and oh, my goodness, what naughty things you write—and then sign my name to them!"

Cathy turned round in surprise. She saw a little thin man bristling with pencils and pens and crayons. They were in rows of pockets, and he even had a row of red pencils in his hat, and some behind his ears. He looked rather like a brownie, she thought.

"I *don't* sign your name!" said Cathy, indignantly. "I don't even know it!"

"My name is Mr. Squiggle," said the little thin man. "And look—here's my name. You've written it three times on this wall!"

He pointed to some funny little squiggles. "See? That's my name—and that, and that. Watch while I sign it and you'll see it's really exactly like my signature."

He scribbled something with one of his pencils—and sure enough it *was* exactly like the three squiggles Cathy had made.

"Well, I didn't know I was signing your name," said Cathy. "It just looks like a squiggle to me."

"Well, it *is*. I told you my name was Squiggle, so, of course, it's a squiggle like that when I write it," said Mr. Squiggle. "And let me tell you this—if some of the things you've

68

said in the squiggle language get known, you'll be in very serious trouble."

"*What* things? I haven't written anything at all!" said Cathy in fright.

"Well, look here—see this?" said Mr. Squiggle, pointing to silly-looking squiggle that Cathy had done on the shed wall. "Do you know what that says in squiggle language? It says, 'I'll smack old Witch Green-Eyes!' Fancy that! Suppose she came along and read that!"

"*I didn't* write that," said Cathy. "I don't even *know* Witch Green-eyes."

"Well, come along and see her," said Mr. Squiggle, pulling at Cathy's arm. "Tell her you didn't mean to write that, so that if she sees it, she won't mind."

"No, thank you," said Cathy, in alarm.

"And look here—see those squiggles?" said Mr. Squiggle, pointing and looking suddenly very fierce. "You've actually written 'The Goblin Long-Nose is always poking his nose into things. It wants pulling.' You're a very rude little girl. I've a good mind to bring Long-Nose here and show him what you've written about him."

"No, don't," said Cathy, almost in tears. "I tell you, I don't know him. Why should I write things about people I don't know?"

"Just part of your silliness, I suppose," said Mr. Squiggle. "I passed through your garden yesterday and what did I see written on your garden seat?"

"What?" asked Cathy, in fright.

"I saw, 'All fairies must keep out of this garden or I'll stamp on their toes!' " said Mr.

Squiggle. "There's a nasty, unkind thing to write!"

Cathy was full of horror. "Did I really write that in squiggle language? I didn't know I had. Oh, I don't want the fairies to keep out of my garden. I'm longing to see one."

"Well, you won't now," said Mr. Squiggle, taking out a big rubber and beginning to rub out some of Cathy's silly squiggles. "Not one will come near you. You're a rude little girl!"

"I'm *not*! I didn't know what I was writing!" wept Cathy. "Have I said anything else dreadful!"

"Good gracious me, yes," said Mr. Squiggle, rubbing out hard. "There was one thing I had to rub out at once, in case you got the Jumping Imps after you. You'd written it on your school playground. You wrote, 'If ever I catch a Jumping Imp I'll slap him and put him in the dustbin!' Fancy being so rude. If I hadn't rubbed that out at once, you'd have had dozens of Jumping Imps giving *you* a few slaps!"

"Was it you who rubbed out what I'd chalked in the playground, then?" said Cathy. "I thought the rain had washed it away."

"I couldn't wait for the rain," said Mr. Squiggle. "It had to be rubbed out at once. You give me a dreadful lot of work. All this rubbing out of rude squiggle messages! I tell you, you'll get into serious trouble one day, writing in the squiggle language! Instead of going round after you and rubbing out, I'll fetch someone like Witch Green-Eyes and let her *read* what you've written. Then she'll be after you."

"I won't write in the squiggle language any more," said Cathy. "Never, never, never. It's dreadful to write rude things without meaning to."

Mr. Squiggle rubbed out the very last scribble. He put his rubber back into his pocket. "I've heard your mother telling you to stop," he said. "And you don't. Look—I'm going to write something in the squiggle language now—watch me!"

And he wrote a lot of quick scribbles. "See

73

what I've written?" he said. " 'Cathy is a rude girl. Give her a smack whenever you go by. Signed, Mr. Squiggle!' "

Then, before Cathy could say another word, he raised his hat to her, making all the pencils in it click together, jumped over the hedge and completely disappeared.

Cathy stared at the squiggles he had written neatly on the shed wall. Did they really mean what he had said? She didn't want to get sly slaps wherever she went! And then, quite suddenly, she felt a sharp little slap on her leg, and

74

someone laughed a high laugh like a blackbird

But there was no one to be seen. Cathy turned to the shed wall. She took out her hanky, wetted it in a nearby rain-barrel, and began to rub out what Mr. Squiggle had written. No more slaps for her!

She didn't get any more slaps—and neither did she scribble any more squiggles. Are you a scribbler, too? Just be careful *you* don't write something rude without meaning to!

THE RAIN

The rain is falling on the hill
    And on the field and lane,
With silver fingers, wet and chill,
    It taps our window-pane!
Pitter-patter, sharp and loud,
    How many drops run by,
Falling from the purple cloud
    Frowning in the sky!

He Wanted Adventures!

THERE was once a boy called Paul who wanted adventures. "If I could have just *one* adventure it would be something!" he thought. "It's so dull at home—just my bicycle to ride, and my electric train to play with, and a shelf full of books."

Well, those weren't dull things at all, of course, but Paul thought they were. "I want to have something really *exciting*," he said. "Something that will make my heart beat fast. An adventure!"

And one day he fell straight into one. He was going down the road when he met the milkman's little horse, running away at top speed! The milkman ran after it shouting. Bottles leapt off the cart and smashed in the road, and what with the sound of galloping hooves and smashing bottles Paul suddenly felt very excited indeed!

The horse galloped straight at him. It had been bitten by a fly and was terrified. Paul took one look and bolted for the hedge.

He squeezed through in a panic, and the horse galloped off down the road. Paul rolled out into the field the other side of the hedge.

He stood up, his heart beating fast. What a narrow escape! The horse might have knocked him over! And then, dear me, he heard a bellow nearby! He turned and saw a big horned animal coming at him, and at the same moment saw a big notice. "Beware of the bull!"

Without waiting another moment Paul fled across the field. Quick! Quick! He must get over the stile before he was tossed by sharp horns!

He fell over the stile, gasping, and rolled right up to two people who were crouching over a fire.

"Here! What are you doing?" said one, angrily. "You've knocked our pail of water over."

So he had. "You go and get us some more out of the stream," said a big boy, much taller than Paul. "Go on—hurry! Coming over the stile like that, right on top of us!"

"The bull was chasing me," said Paul.

"Fibber!" said the other boy.

"I shan't get you any water if you call me that," said Paul, annoyed.

"Oh yes you will," said the big boy, and he caught hold of Paul. He put the pail over his head and then he and the other boy marched him to the stream.

"Now then—fill the pail with water," said the big boy. But Paul wouldn't.

Splash! He found himself in the stream! The other boy had given him a sharp push.

They both roared with delight to see Paul scramble out the other side, wet through. He thought they were going to jump the stream and chase him, so he set off at top speed to where the stream ran into the river.

There was a boat there. Paul leapt into it, his heart thumping madly. He pushed off and began rowing. Thank goodness he had got away from those awful boys.

An angry voice yelled at him. "Hey, you!

What are you doing, taking my boat? Bring it
back at once."

Paul tried to swing it round, and somehow
an oar got entangled in some weed. Paul
leaned out to get it free—and over he went,
splash into the water a second time!

He was so afraid of the shouting man that
he didn't swim the little way to the bank he had
left—he tried to swim right across the wide
river. He couldn't, of course, and soon he was
yelling for help.

"Help! I shall drown! Help!"

A river steamer came up, heard his cries,

and stopped near by. A boat-hook was put out
and the hook caught his clothes. He was pulled
near the steamer and hauled aboard. Soon he
was telling everyone what had happened—from
the moment he had met the runaway horse to
now.

"My!" said a boy, enviously, "what a fine
lot of adventures you've had! I wish I'd been
you!"

"Adventures!" said Paul. "Were those *adventures*? I hated them. I've always wanted adventures—but not that kind!"

"Ah—they might have been fine if you'd
managed them all right," said the boy. "You
ran away from them all."

"How do you *manage* adventures?" said Paul,
surprised.

"Well—the milkman's pony is very small—
you could easily have caught his reins and
pulled him to a standstill," said the boy. "Then
everyone would have cheered you and said how
brave you were. But you ran away. Then, you
know, there *isn't* a bull in that field, although
there's a notice there. I know, because it
belongs to my father, who's a farmer."

"There *was* a bull. I saw its horns," said Paul.

"That was Buttercup, our old cow," said the boy. "She's quite harmless. I expect she wondered why you scrambled through the hedge like that. If you'd said 'Shoo!' to her, she would have run off with her tail in the air, and you'd have thought you'd scared a bull, and felt very brave."

"But I ran away," said Paul, mournfully,

83

"and bumped into a picnic party of two boys and upset their pail."

"Yes. Those two boys are camping there. They are the Prince of Bigtonia and his cousin," said the boy. "They would have asked you to share their meal and made friends with you if you hadn't been so silly. Why couldn't you have said you were sorry and gone to get them more water at once? They'd have made friends with you then."

"But I struggled and they threw me into the stream," said Paul. "*I* didn't know who they were. I've heard of the Prince—he's a wonderful cricketer, isn't he? I'd love to meet him."

"Well, you did—and you ran away from that adventure, too," said the boy. "And you took a boat—it was my uncle's, you know, I recognized him yelling on the bank. He'd have let you use his boat any day, and you and I could have gone rowing together."

"But I upset the boat, and got dragged aboard this steamer," said poor Paul. "And everyone is laughing at me."

"Well—run away again," said the boy. "Jump overboard! I tell you, you don't know

how to manage adventures! You can get a lot
out of them if you face up to and manage them
in the right way. My word, I'd love adventures.
You're a duffer. You've had plenty today, and
all you can say is that you hated them. Pooh—
what a baby you are!"

Well, Paul got off the steamer at the next
stop and went home in soaking wet clothes. He
was afraid that his next adventure would be a
spanking from his father for coming home with
torn and dripping clothes! The boat-hook had
made a great hole in his shorts.

"Adventures! Perhaps I *might* have liked them if I hadn't run away all the time," said Paul. "I'll *manage* them next time, like that boy said. But oh, dear—if Dad is my next adventure, I don't know *how* I'm going to manage him!"

I don't either—it's not the kind of adventure anyone likes, is it?

WAKING UP

The frogs in the pond were all soundly asleep;
One woke, and put up his small head to peep.
"It's spring-time," he cried, and gave such a
                       loud croak,
That all the frogs stirred in the mud and awoke!

They swam and they wriggled, they kicked out
                       their legs,
They croaked and they gambolled, and laid
                       lots of eggs,
Then out of the pond they all scrambled in glee,
And went to catch flies for their dinner and tea!

The Big Dog

ONE day a very big dog came running into the gates of Green Hedges. He was an ugly dog and a fierce one, and Bobs the puppy didn't like the look of him at all. The dog ran to the porch and ate up the cat's dinner. He ran to the pigeon bowl and crunched up the pigeon seed. He then went to the pond for a drink and drank so much that Bobs was really afraid he would empty the pond.

For four days the big ugly dog came, and none of the animals at Green Hedges dared to stop him. At last they held a meeting about it, and everybody said his say.

"He's a wicked dog and ought to be stopped," said Bobs.

"He's a perfect nuisance, and we really *must* do something!" said Sandy.

"I would scratch him if I could get near him," said Cosy.

"And I would nip his tail if he didn't wag it so fast," said Pitapat.

"What you should do is get an old muzzle and strap it on his mouth," said Bimbo the kitten, who always talked a great deal and very loudly, too. "You should stop him from eating things, then he wouldn't get my dinner or the pigeon's cither. You should . . ."

"You are full of good ideas, Bimbo," said Bobs, politely. "But you talk too much. Also, we are not deaf, though you seem to think we are."

"Well, you are stupid, and I have to shout to get any good ideas into your head," said Bimbo rudely. "I tell you, Bobs, my idea is

best of all—muzzle the dog and he will do no more harm."

"Very well," said Bobs. "We will carry out your idea. Sandy, fetch that old muzzle from the rubbish heap next door. Bimbo, as it's your idea, you shall muzzle the dog yourself. Look, here's the muzzle—and there's the big dog just coming in at the gate! Hurry up and go to him before he eats your dinner again!"

Everyone looked at Bimbo, and he began to swing his tail crossly. Whatever was he to do?

"Take the muzzle quickly," said Bobs, grinning.

"Well, I will go and muzzle that big dog," said Bimbo at last. "I am a very brave kitten. You are all cowards, because you dare not muzzle him." He took up the muzzle and started off towards the dog. Then he looked back and said: "I can put the muzzle on by myself, but I am not big enough to hold the dog still whilst I strap it on. Will you come and hold the dog for me, Bobs?"

"Er—er—I've a little job to do for Mistress!" said Bobs, and he rushed away.

"Will *you* come and hold the dog for me, Sandy?" asked Bimbo. But Sandy suddenly remembered that he had a bone to see to, and he was gone.

"Will *you* hold the dog for me?" Bimbo asked Cosy and Pitapat. But they shook their heads and said they had promised to go and meet the milkman. So Bimbo was left all alone. He grinned to himself and dropped the muzzle into the pond.

"Well, I can't muzzle the dog if nobody will help me!" he shouted in his loudest voice—and then he ran for his life! The big dog had seen him and Bimbo was not going to stop and say good morning.

After that nobody mentioned big dogs again, and I'm not surprised, are you?

THE FRIENDLY TOAD

I am a toad, a friendly thing,
    I eat your slugs and flies,
I know I'm ugly, brown and squat—
    But have you seen my eyes?
Just look at them—like jewels rare,
    Gleaming in my head,
I watch you with them as I sit
    Upon your garden bed.
Please like me, little boy and girl,
    I can't help how I grew,
I've got to be a toad, you know,
    And *you*'ve got to be *you*!

The Great Big Bone!
(A Story by Bobs the Dog)

ONCE upon a time, dear children, as I was out walking, I smelt a glorious smell. I stopped and sniffed. It was a smell of Bone, and it came from the hedge.

"Tails and Whiskers!" I wuffed to myself. "It must be a great big bone to have such a great big smell." So I ran to find it—and just exactly at the same moment as I came from *my* side of the hedge, another dog, much smaller than I am, ran to get that bone from the *other* side of the hedge.

"It's *my* bone!" I growled.

"No, it's *mine*!" growled the other dog. He took one end and I took the other, and we snarled like the beginning of a thunderstorm. It was a wonderful bone, with meat on it, and it certainly had a wonderful smell.

"Do you know, dog, I believe this bone's bad," suddenly said the other dog to me, and he dropped his end and began to sniff along it. "It's been here a long time, and I shouldn't be surprised if it's poisonous now. Once I ate a

poisoned fish-head and I was dreadfully ill. I couldn't wag my tail for three weeks."

I dropped my end too and sniffed. That bone had a glorious smell, but it certainly was very strong indeed. I wondered if it *could* be bad. I can tell you, I didn't want to lose the wag out of *my* tail, it's too useful.

"Shall I taste the bone and *see* if it's all right?" said the little dog.

"If you like," I said. So the dog ran his tongue over it and bit a piece of meat off. And then, whiskers and tails, dear children, he

D
93

suddenly rolled over and over, gave dreadful yelps of pain and wuffed: "Oh, fetch help, fetch help! I'm poisoned!"

I was frightened, I can tell you. "Lie there, dog," I said. "I'll go and fetch my Mistress. She will know how to make you better."

"Oh, quick, oh, quick!" groaned the little dog, rolling over and over again. "Oh, who would have thought that bone was so poisonous!"

I rushed off as fast as my four paws could go. I hunted everywhere for Mistress, and at last I found her.

"Come quickly!" I begged her. "There's a poor little dog in great pain through eating a poisoned bone."

So Mistress put on her coat and hurried off with me to the hedge. "He's just about here," I said. I scurried to the hedge—but wags and whistles, would you believe it, there was no little dog there—and no bone either! They were both gone, and all that was left was a wonderful smell of faraway bone!

"He was too little to fight you for that bone!" chuckled a robin in the hedge. "But quite big enough to trick you! Trilla, trilla, what a duffer you are!"

And, dear children, I had no wag in my tail all that day, I was so upset. Just wait till I meet that little dog again!

The Vowel Dolls

MISS BROWN, the teacher, was teaching her children the names of the five letters that we call the vowels. She wrote them up on the board.

"Here they are," she said, "A-E-I-O-U. Now we will see who knows them all tomorrow morning. They are the letters that help all the others to speak!"

"Oh dear!" said Anna. "I know I shall never learn them! I am so bad at remembering!"

So she was! Anna found it very difficult to remember poetry, or tables or songs, though she did try very hard.

"Well, Anna," said Miss Brown, "I wish you could give us all a surprise tomorrow morning and say the names of the five vowels without a single mistake!"

Anna ran home, thinking hard. It *would* be fun to give everyone a surprise. How could she do it? But by the time Anna had got home the little girl had already forgotten all the five vowels! She was ready to cry.

"What's the matter?" asked Mother.

"I did want to remember the five vowels that Miss Brown put on the board this morning," said Anna. "And now I have forgotten them!"

"Well, *I* know them," said Mother. "A-E-I-O-U!"

"Oh, thank you, Mother," said Anna. She ran to her toy-cupboard and pulled out her dolls. She was looking for Amy, her oldest doll. Ah, there she was!

"A for Amy—you're the first vowel, Amy!" said Anna. "Now, where is Edith? Oh, here you are Edith, in your dress of blue silk. E for

97

Edith—you are the second vowel. Sit beside Amy. Now for Ivy. Oh dear, where's Ivy?"

Ivy was an old rag doll with only one arm. Anna found her at last and sat her beside Edith. "I for Ivy!" she said. "You are the third vowel, Ivy. Now, where is the fourth one—O?"

There didn't seem any doll for the vowel O, but at last Anna found a little Swedish boy-doll called Olaf. She pulled him out in glee.

"You will do nicely, Olaf!" she said. "O for Olaf—you are the fourth vowel. Sit beside Ivy. Now where is Una, my baby doll? Here she is the darling! U for Una—you are the fifth vowel, Una!"

There were all the dolls, sitting in a row— Amy, Edith, Ivy, Olaf and Una. Anna pointed to them one by one—"A, E, I, O, U!" she said. "Now, if I remember you all sitting there side by side, and think of your names, I shall remember the vowels!"

The next morning, when Miss Brown asked who remembered the five vowels of the alphabet, how surprised she was to see Anna's hand shoot up at once.

THE VOWEL DOLLS

"*You*, Anna?" she said in astonishment. "Well—see if you can say them!"

Anna thought of her five dolls sitting at home in a row. "A—" she said, thinking of Amy. "E-I-O-U!"

"Well done, Anna!" said the teacher. "Do tell me how you managed to remember them so well?"

"My dolls taught me!" said Anna.

"Bring them to school and let them teach the others too!" said the teacher.

And what do you think? Anna brought her dolls to school the next day, and sat them up in a row—and there they all are, Amy, Edith, Ivy, Olaf and Una, teaching the children the names of the five vowels!

"A Lark in a Cage . . ."

ONCE upon a time a dog, chained up in a yard, longed for a drink. He went to his bowl, but it was empty. It had been empty for two days and no one had thought about it. So the dog howled. But there was nobody who bothered to listen to his cry.

Once upon a time there was a cat that nobody wanted, so it had no home. It could not

find enough food to eat, and it grew thin and ill.
Its fur fell off. It lay on a wall and mewed piti-
fully for help. But there was nobody who
bothered to listen to its cry.

Once upon a time there was a gentle pony
who belonged to a hard master. He worked the
pony each day till the animal could hardly stand.
But he was a willing creature, and did not shirk
his work or hate his master. The man was bad-
tempered, and struck the pony. Then the pony
lifted his head and cried out, not for less work,
or better food, but for a kind word and a little
love. But there was nobody who bothered to
listen to his cry.

Once upon a time there was a wild lark that
someone had caught and put into a tiny cage.
The lark beat its wings against the bars, and
sang its heart out for the open fields and the
blue sky. But there was nobody who bothered
to understand its cry.

And then one day there came a boy who
heard the dog howling and wondered why. He
saw the empty bowl and was sorry. He took it
and filled it with water for the dog. The dog
drank eagerly and licked the boy's hand. Ah,

here was someone with ears and eyes at last!

And then a little girl saw the cat on the wall, and heard it mewing. She too had eyes and ears and an understanding heart. She told her mother, and they took the cat home. They fed it and cared for it—and the stray cat repaid them with love.

And what about the pony? Two children heard his mournful neighing, and looked into his stable. When they saw his sorrowful brown eyes they knew he was sad. They fetched him a handful of the rich green grass he loved, and the boy saved him a lump of sugar from his own tea. They gave him loving words and stroked his nose whenever they passed. Then the pony knew there was kindness in the world after all, and he was glad.

The lark in its tiny cage was almost dead with fright and misery, but it still sang. A little girl heard it one day and listened unhappily, for

she understood its wild song. She opened her moneybox. She took out all the pennies there and she bought the lark in its cage. She opened the little door and took the lark out. It stretched its wings and rose into the air, singing madly. Ah, to think there had been someone who understood its wild and sorrowful song!

And what were the names of these children who had eyes to see and ears to hear, and hearts to understand? They were the names of any child in the world who has pity and love in his heart for other creatures—*your* name, perhaps, for you, too, would hear and answer any pitiful cry. Yes—we will give the children *your* name, for maybe it was you who freed the lark, and saved the cat, gave water to the dog and kindness to the pony!

(Can *you* write a story about some unhappy animal and tell how you came along and helped it?)

The Horse, the Wasp and the Donkey

ONCE upon a time a red, ripe apple fell from an old apple tree into a ditch below. Plop! it went, and lay there, bright and glowing. The brown horse that lived in the field saw it and galloped up to it eagerly, for he loved an apple—but someone else had seen it, too—and that someone was a wasp, striped in yellow and black.

The wasp had found few apples, for it was a bad year for fruit. So when she saw this juicy, red one, she was delighted. She flew down to it just exactly at the same moment as the brown horse galloped up to eat it.

"It's mine!" buzzed the wasp, angrily.

"I saw it first!" neighed the horse, in a rage.

"I'll sting you if you eat my apple!" said the wasp, and the horse saw her long sting quivering at the end of her body.

"I'll eat you and the apple, too, if you dare to suck the juice!" cried the horse, who was longing to munch that red apple.

"Now, now, what's all this?" said another voice, and up trotted the grey donkey. "What are you quarrelling about? Can I help you to settle your quarrel?"

"*You!*" cried the horse and the wasp, together. "Whoever heard of a stupid donkey settling a quarrel? You haven't enough brains!"

The donkey didn't seem to mind their rudeness. "Well, tell me what your quarrel is about," he said.

So the horse told him. The donkey flicked his long tail and brayed with laughter.

"How foolish you both are!" he said. "You could easily settle your quarrel if you would do what I say. Why don't you both go to the other end of the field, and then, starting off together, see who can reach the apple first? Whoever wins the race has the apple!"

"That seems a good idea," said the horse, who felt certain he could race the little wasp.

"I agree," said the wasp, who was sure she could fly far faster than the clumsy old horse could run.

"Off you go, then, to the end of the field," said the donkey. "When I bray, start to run, horse, and fly, wasp!" The two went off, the wasp buzzing excitedly and the horse flicking his tail. When they reached the end of the field, the donkey lifted up his head and brayed loudly. At once the horse began to gallop and the wasp began to fly at top speed.

They arrived at the ditch at the very same moment—but what a strange thing, the apple was gone! Yes, no matter where they looked, it wasn't there! They looked round for the donkey—and *he* was gone, too! The gate was open and there was no sign of that little grey donkey.

"He wasn't so stupid as he looked," said the horse, suddenly.

"No," said the wasp, angrily. "*We* were the stupid ones! We could easily have shared that apple between us. Now there is none to share. *I* know why that donkey has disappeared!"

So do I. Do you?

The Wrong Berries

ONCE upon a time there was a girl called Minnie, who wanted to go and be nurse to children because she loved them. But her mother said no, she must go and work in a shop.

"But I don't like the town," said Minnie. "I like the country and the birds and flowers. Let me go and be nurse to country children, mother."

But it was no good. Minnie had to go and work in a shop. She had an afternoon free once a week which she always spent wandering in the country. And it was on one of these afternoons that she saw the two little children.

They were twins and were dressed alike in brown overalls. They were wandering along by the hedge, picking berries and flowers. At first Minnie thought they were blackberrying—and then saw that they were picking the purple privet berries and eating them.

She ran up to them and took the berries from them. "You mustn't eat those!" she said.

"They will make you ill! What else have you eaten?"

The children showed her. They had eaten some of the pink spindle-berries with their bright orange seeds, a few white snowberries, some red holly berries, and two or three of the pretty pink berries of the yew.

"We eat blackberries," they said, "so why shouldn't we eat these? They are prettier than blackberries."

"Pretty berries are the worst to eat," said Minnie. "Didn't your mother tell you not to eat all those berries? Or didn't you learn at school?"

"We don't go to school," said the twins. "And our mother is too busy to tell us things like that. Oh! we do feel ill!"

Minnie was worried. They were such dear little children, and perhaps they would be poisoned now. She picked one up under each arm and carried them to her home. Her mother was out, so she popped them into her own bed, gave them some salt and water and then a drink of warm milk. Then she sent a neighbour for the doctor.

Well, those children were dreadfully ill, poor little things, and the doctor said they mustn't be moved. They were too ill even to say who they were—but it wasn't long before Minnie found out! They were the twin son and daughter of the lovely Princess Mirabelle, who was staying in the castle nearby. They had wandered out of the gardens when their nurse was not looking!

The nurse and the princess hurried to Minnie's cottage when they heard what had

happened. The nurse was pale because she knew she would never be trusted again. The Princess was crying because she was afraid her twins would never get better.

"Don't you worry, Madam," said Minnie. "I'll nurse them for you. I'm fond of children, and I'll sit up day and night with them."

For a whole week Minnie nursed the twins, and at last she got them well. She had lost her job in the shop, and her mother was angry with her—but what do you think the Princess said?

"I can't thank you enough, Minnie," she said. "Will you be the twins' nurse? You are very young, but you are loving and sensible!"

Well, of course, it was just what Minnie wanted most in the world! Back to the castle she went with the twins, as happy as could be.

"Fancy!" she said. "I never thought that learning about poisonous berries would bring me such a fine reward!" But she really deserved it, didn't she?

The Old Red Stocking

THERE was once a pair of red stockings, long and warm. They belonged to Lucy Brown, and she wore them when she went skating.

But one day she fell down and made such an enormous hole in the knee of one stocking that her mother said she really couldn't mend it. So Lucy took the stockings to old Mrs. Jones, who cobbled up the hole and wore the stockings herself. She was very pleased with them.

The stockings were pleased, too. They didn't want to be used as floor-cloths, for they were not very old. So they were delighted to find that old Mrs. Jones liked them so much.

She wore them and wore them and wore them. She washed them every week and put them on again. And one day when they were drying over the fire, one of the red stockings fell into the grate. It caught fire, and at once a dreadful smell of burning filled the kitchen. Mrs. Jones smelt it and hurried to the fire. She snatched up the stocking, but alas! all the foot had been burnt out of it.

"Oh dear, oh dear!" said Mrs. Jones, sadly. "That's no use at all now—and I was so pleased with those red stockings, too. I'll have to use them for floor-rags."

Poor red stockings! The one that was burnt was used that very day to wash over the floor— but the other one was put away in a drawer until it was needed as a floor-cloth. It was very sad to be alone, and it trembled every time the drawer was opened in case the time had come for it to be used as a rag.

But old Mrs. Jones found another use for it.

She saved up her money each week—and she suddenly thought how nice it would be to put it all into the old red stocking! So she took out the stocking, slipped all her pennies and sixpences into it and hid it at the back of a cupboard.

The stocking was pleased. The pennies and sixpences had so many tales to tell, and the stocking liked hearing them. It liked keeping all the money safe too—it felt important. It wouldn't be used for a floor-cloth now!

But, dear me, that summer a little clothes-moth crept into the cupboard and laid its eggs in the stocking—and when the eggs hatched into grubs they ate holes all the way up the red stocking, so that when old Mrs. Jones took it out to count up her money at Christmas time, some of the little sixpenny bits fell out of the holes!

"Dear, dear, the stocking is moth-eaten!" said Mrs. Jones. "I'll have to keep my money somewhere else. The stocking shall be used for a rag."

She put it on the shelf to use that afternoon —but at dinner time her little grand-daughter ran in to see her, and she spied the stocking.

"Oh, Granny!" she said. "It's Christmas Eve tonight, and I'm going to hang up my sock —but it's dreadfully small; so do you think you would lend me that lovely old red stocking to hang up? It would hold much more than my little sock!"

"Of course, Mollie!" said Mrs. Jones, and she gave the child the stocking. And wasn't it just delighted? Fancy being used for a Christmas stocking! What luck!

And on Christmas morning it was full of toys for Mollie—a long, knobbly, red stocking. It *was* exciting. What do you suppose happened to it next? Perhaps *you* can make up the rest of its adventures!

Tom's Mackintosh

TOM was really rather a monkey. He was the sort of boy who thinks it is just a waste of time to wear gum-boots on a wet morning, a coat on a cold morning, or gloves on a frosty one. As for putting on a mackintosh in case it should rain, well, Tom would never think of such a sensible thing.

So, of course, his mother had to think of it for him! She was always saying, "Tom, have you got your coat on? Tom, take your mack, it's going to rain. Tom, where is your scarf on this cold morning?" and things like that. Perhaps your mother says them to you, too.

Now Tom loved his mother and tried to please her—but he *did* grumble so. "I don't *want* to wear a coat today!" he would say. "Oh bother scarves and hats and gloves! Oh, Mother, *don't* make me wear my mack!"

One day his mother was ill and she couldn't see him off to school as she usually did. She looked at the sky through the window, and she saw that it was very cloudy. So when Tom

came in to kiss her goodbye she said, "Tom, put your mack on, there's a good boy. It's going to rain."

Tom pouted. Tom sulked. Macks were a nuisance. Macks were useless. Macks were too long and too tight, and too everything else. So his mother at last lay back in bed and said sadly, "Well, do as you please, if you feel like that. I'm too tired to say any more."

Tom ran downstairs pleased. Now he

needn't put his mack on—but as he ran out of the door he felt mean. Yes—he *would* wear it— just to please his mother, though he felt quite sure the sun was going to shine.

And it did shine, too, all the morning. Tom came out of school carrying his mack, wishing he had left it at home after all. He ran along by the canal on his way home—and suddenly he saw some children shouting by the bank. He ran up to see what was the matter.

"Ann's fallen in! Ann's fallen in! Where's a rope?"

Somebody ran up with a rope. They threw it to Ann—but, alas, it was not long enough. Now, what should they do? None of the children could swim, and there was no grown-up anywhere near. Tom stared in horror, for he was very fond of Ann.

And then a splendid idea came to him! What about the belt of his mack? If he took it off, tied it to the end of the rope and threw it to Ann, it would then be long enough to reach her! He tore the belt from his mack, quickly knotted it to the short rope, and then threw rope and belt to poor, struggling Ann. She caught hold

of the belt before she went under the water again—and Tom hauled on the rope strongly, with the others helping him.

Ann was drawn to the bank, wet, cold and sobbing. Tom hurried her to his home to dry her by the fire. Then he tore upstairs to his mother.

"Mother! Ann fell into the canal, and the rope was too short to reach her. So I used my mackintosh belt as well, and that saved her. Oh, Mother, wasn't it a good thing you made me take my mack!"

"Wasn't it a good thing I had a boy who did as he was told?" said his mother, delighted. "If you hadn't taken your mack, Ann would have been drowned. Your obedience to me saved her life, Tom! I'm proud of you!"

You're a Bully!

"Stop it, Jerry! You're hurting!" said William, trying to wriggle away from the big boy who was holding him.

"Coward!" said Jerry, and held William still more tightly.

"*You're* the coward!" said William. "Just because you're so much bigger and stronger

than the rest of us, you think you can do what you like. Oooooh! Stop it! You'll break my arm!"

The other children came running up just then, and Jerry let go William's arms. William rubbed them hard, and glared at Jerry. "You're a bully! You want a jolly good whipping! Always lying in wait for us and trying your nasty little tricks!"

Jerry made a step towards William as if he was going to catch him again, but the other children closed round, looking so fierce that Jerry changed his mind. Like most bullies, he was a coward at heart. He laughed loudly, and stalked off.

"Not one of you dares to stand up to me!" he jeered. "You're a lot of cowards."

The others watched him go. He was a great big boy, as tall as a man, although he was only fourteen. Nobody liked him. He teased the girls, he frightened the small ones, and he ill-treated the big ones.

"Don't you think we'd better tell the Headmaster about him?" said Susan, at last. "I know it's telling tales, but surely there are times when it's *right* to tell a tale?"

"Or couldn't we tell our mothers and fathers?" said Graham, a small boy who was really very scared of Jerry.

"I told mine," said Rita, "and Mother went to complain to Jerry's mother. And Jerry's mother was rude to her, and I haven't been able to buy any ice-creams or sweets at her shop since then!"

Jerry's mother kept a sweet-shop, and as it was the only one in the village it was very important to the children. There was a long silence after this statement from Rita. Nobody wanted to go without sweets or ice-creams.

"Jerry hasn't got a father to keep him in order," said Tom. "He just does what he likes. *My* father is jolly strict, and I just wish Jerry had a father like him!"

"Your father's nice," said Alice. "He may be strict, but he keeps all his promises to you, and he takes you about a lot. I like your father."

"What are we going to do about Jerry, though?" said Susan. "He took the ribbons off my plaits yesterday and I know he won't give them back."

"And he snatched little Mary's biscuits from her," said Kenneth. "I tried to get them back, but he just gave me a push and over I went. He's as strong as a giant!"

"We've talked and talked about Jerry for months," said Graham. "But we never *do* anything because there is nothing to be done—except sneak about him. I feel as if I'm going to sneak jolly soon if he doesn't change his ways! I hate to see him tease my little sister."

"*He* won't change his ways!" said Pam.

"People like Jerry never do—unless they meet someone bigger and stronger and fiercer than themselves! Then they're afraid."

"I wish he *could* meet someone bigger and fiercer than he is!" said Jack, gloomily. "But he never will!"

"Well—never mind—let's forget him and go and have a game," said William. "Goodness, my arms hurt. Jerry really is hateful!"

The children all went off to the field to play. Stuck to a tree by the gate was a big notice, and they all stood round to read it.

"Mr. Galliano's Circus is
COMING!
See Lotta and Jimmy
and
Lucky the Wonder Dog!
Elephants, Chimpanzees, Bears,
Dancing Horses
and
BOO-BOO the GIANT.
Grand Circus
presented by the great
Mr. Galliano!"

"I say! Galliano's Circus is coming again!" said William, in delight. "We must see it!"

He went home to tell his mother about the circus. She laughed.

"You'll be able to go as many times as you like," she said. "Boo-Boo the Giant is with it— and he's a second cousin of mine! He'll be coming here to meals, I expect."

What a bit of news! William could hardly believe it. But what his mother said was quite true—Boo-Boo *was* her cousin, and he did go to William's house for many meals.

He looked quite different in William's home from when he was in the circus! In the circus he was twelve feet tall, because he walked on stilts, and wore a great giant-head over his own. He would have been a very frightening person there if he hadn't been so full of fun and silly tricks.

But in William's home he didn't look a giant at all. He was just about as tall as William's father, and his head was the ordinary size, of course. He was a merry, kind fellow, and the whole family laughed at his jokes. William loved him.

One day William came home looking white. Boo-Boo was there and looked at him in surprise.

"What's up?" he said. "Do you feel ill?"

"A bit sick, that's all," said William. "A fellow at our school took my chair away just as I was going to sit down. He's always doing that. I hurt my back, I sat down on the floor with such a bump."

"Children who do that ought to be well and truly whipped," said Boo-Boo. "What a nasty piece of work that boy must be!"

"He is," said William. "He's a bully. He scares the younger ones till they're afraid to go home unless about twenty of them go together! But his mother keeps the sweet-shop, you see, so we don't like to make too much fuss."

"What he wants is someone to scare him as much as he scares others," said Boo-Boo. "That's the best cure for bullies. A terrible fright!"

"Yes. But he's big and strong, so we none of us can stand up to him," said William.

Boo-Boo gave William a sudden wink, and leaned over to whisper in his ear. "What about a giant like me lying in wait for him?" he said. "You could tell me where to lie in wait, couldn't you? I could talk to Jerry all right!"

William stared at Boo-Boo, his eyes suddenly bright. "Oh, Boo-Boo, that would be a most *wonderful* idea!" he said. "Oh, please do! Jerry deserves a punishment like that!"

"Right. You plan it with your friends, and I'll get my giant's rig-out—head and stilts and all—and dress up," said Boo-Boo. "And then Master Jerry will have the fright of his life!"

"He hasn't been to the circus," said William. "So he won't have seen you. He's scared of the bears and the chimpanzees. But bullies are always cowards, aren't they?"

"Always," said Boo-Boo. "Now, you go and tell your friends, and make your plans."

It didn't take long for a few plans to be made, as you can guess. All the children were thrilled.

"Jerry always goes to fetch eggs from Mrs. Straw's farm, through the wood every Tuesday night," said Susan. "Could Boo-Boo lie in wait for him there?"

"And he goes to the cinema every Wednesday," said Kenneth. "Boo-Boo could wait for him under those trees near the cinema."

"Yes! And couldn't he chase him over the fields on the night he goes to see his aunt?" said Rita. "I always see him passing then, on Thursday evenings. I don't see him now, of course, because the evenings are dark—but I know he goes to his aunt in Churchin Lane each Thursday."

Boo-Boo was told all this, and grinned. "Right! I'll wait in the wood tomorrow night, Tuesday," he said. "You can watch, if you like, and show me where it's best to hide."

So, the next night, Boo-Boo and seven or eight children went quietly into the wood. The moon was just coming up so there was a little light to see by. The children showed Boo-Boo a good place to hide, and then went off behind the trees.

Soon Jerry came along, whistling loudly, for he was always afraid of the dark. Just as he got to a big oak-tree a great voice boomed at him.

"Ho! So YOU'RE the boy who bullies, are you? HO, HO, HO! Let me get at you!"

And, to Jerry's great horror, a most enormous figure came out from behind the tree, looking huge in the moonlight. It was Boo-Boo, of course. But Jerry didn't know that. He gave a scream and fled.

Boo-Boo chased him on his stilts, and would have caught him if his head hadn't kept knocking against the tree-branches! Jerry ran all the way home, screaming that a giant was after him, a giant as tall as the trees!

His mother didn't believe him, of course, and for once in a way was angry with him. But Jerry wouldn't go out again to fetch the eggs.

Next day Jerry began to think he had imagined it all—but all the same he made up a wonderful story to tell the others!

"On my way to the farm last night, a great giant-fellow attacked me," he boasted. "And I let fly at him and knocked him down flat—just like this!" And he hit out at poor Kenneth and made him fall across a desk.

"You be careful the giant doesn't come after you again!" said Rita.

Well, he did, of course, the very next night!

As Jerry was on his way to the cinema that night, something appeared from the shadow of the trees and Jerry gazed in horror. It was the giant that had chased him the night before! He yelled and ran away at top speed.

He ran down the quiet lane, and this time it was easy for Boo-Boo to chase him, because there were no trees to stop him. He was on stilts, so he couldn't go as fast as Jerry—but suddenly the boy tripped and fell, and lay on the ground yelling, so frightened that he couldn't get up.

Boo-Boo came up to him, and once more an enormous voice boomed out.

"So you said you'd fought me and knocked me down, did you? Get up, and we'll have a proper fight! This time you can fight one nearer your own size, instead of little girls, and small boys. Get up, I say! You play the giant to your school-mates, don't you—well, I'll play the giant to *you*, and my word, there won't be much of you left!"

Jerry looked up and saw the great figure towering above him. He leapt up suddenly and tore into the hedge, sobbing.

But some of the boys and girls were there hiding, and William caught hold of Jerry. Jerry quite thought another giant must be there and he wrenched himself away and raced home, crying.

He hardly dared to go out the next night, but he knew his aunt had a present for him, so he went. He kept a sharp look-out for the giant. He hadn't dared to boast about him to the others that day. In fact, he had been very quiet, very gloomy, and hadn't teased or hurt anyone. What a change!

He went cautiously over the field to the lane where his aunt lived, keeping a good look-out—and, oh my, just as he was half-way across, somebody suddenly got up from the grass—and there was the giant again, towering above him. This time he had Jerry by the arm.

"Ah! The bully again! What shall I do with you? The same as you do to others? A good idea, don't you think so?"

He had Jerry's arm in such a tight grip that

141

the boy yelled. Now he knew what it was like when he gripped others and hurt them.

"Shall I pull your hair?" boomed Boo-Boo. "Or sit on you hard and bounce up and down like you do to the others? Or have you any other good ideas to tell me?"

Jerry fell down on his knees. "Please let me go! I promise faithfully I'll never bully the others again. I promise you. Oh, let me go, let me go!"

Boo-Boo still held him hard, bending down over the kneeling boy. "Bullies don't keep their word. Cowards don't keep their word, and you are both. No, no—you come with me and I'll show you what happens in my land to people like you!"

And then something extraordinary happened. William, who had been watching with the others, suddenly felt terribly sorry for the shivering, shaking Jerry. He ran out to him, and pulled him away from Boo-Boo.

"That's enough!" he cried loudly. "Let him go now. He's almost scared out of his wits!"

And, to Jerry's enormous relief, Boo-Boo the giant went swiftly away over the fields on his long, long legs. He caught hold of William, sobbing.

"Oh, William, you are brave! You saved me! I'm so scared."

"Yes—just as scared as we've often been of you, Jerry," said William. "Get up and stop howling. I heard your promise to that giant. Are you going to keep it?"

"Yes. Oh, yes," said Jerry, getting up. "You would tell that giant if I didn't keep it, wouldn't you?"

"I might," said William. "But I should think you've learnt your lesson. You're a coward, Jerry. We've all watched you being a coward, and we've all heard your promise. Look —here come the others from behind the hedge."

Jerry stared at them in the moonlight, still too scared to wonder why William and the others happened to be there. He caught hold of William's arm again, as the moon went in and everything became dark.

"You came out and saved me, William," he said. "You were very brave. I would have thought you hated me too much to save me."

"I was sorry for you," said William. "It

was silly of me, perhaps, but I couldn't help it.
Come on—let's get back home now. It's late."

You'll want to know what happened to
Jerry after that. Well, that was the end of his
being a bully. Boo-Boo had scared him out of
his horrid ways—but William's little bit of
kindness had made him ashamed of them, too.

And now the children get a lot more sweets
than ever they did before, because Jerry has
suddenly turned generous, and begs them from
his mother for all his friends. Did I say *friends*?
Yes, I did—and that just shows you how different
Jerry is!

The Quarrel in the Playroom

JENNY, Thea and Dick came into their playroom, talking. They were just back from morning school. The toys looked at them eagerly, and listened, because it was always such fun to hear what the children said.

"Fancy! Miss Brown is giving a tea-party for our *toys!*" said little Jenny. "I've never taken

any of my toys out to a tea-party before, though we've often given them parties here at home."

"And Miss Brown has got three prizes—for the nicest doll, bear or golliwog there—or any other toy," said Thea, looking round at the toys. "We've got some nice toys. One of them might win a prize."

"A bear might win a prize," said Dick. "Or a monkey. Or even a toy cat or dog. We'll have to decide which are our nicest toys before we go tomorrow."

Well, as you can imagine, the toys listened to all this in the greatest excitement! A tea-party given specially for them by Miss Brown! And prizes for the nicest ones! How very, very proud they would be if they came home with a prize to show all the other toys!

When the children had gone to bed that night, what an excitement there was among the toys. How they chattered and ran about! The curly-haired doll with the big blue eyes and the blue silk dress to match was very excited indeed. She was sure she would be taken to the party by Jenny, and she was even more sure that she would win a prize!

"I'm so pretty," she said, walking about so that her silk frock went swish-swish-swish. "And everyone loves my lovely hair. It's real, you know. And I show my teeth so nicely when I smile."

"Don't be so conceited," said the big golliwog, crossly. "And stop swishing about round and round the room. You make a draught whenever you pass me."

"Poor golly!" said the curly-haired doll, in a pitying voice. "So black and so cross always! *You* won't win a prize. In fact, I don't expect anyone will take you to the party."

147

"They will!" said the golliwog at once. "She loves me. She says I'm the blackest golliwog that ever was, and my clothes are very, very fine. I shall win the golliwog prize, if there is one."

"Stop boasting," said the big teddy bear, and he pressed himself in the middle so that he gave a deep growl and made everyone jump. "I heard Dick say that *I* was to be taken, anyway, and as neither of you have growls I'm pretty certain I'll walk off with any prize that goes to our three children. Grrrrrr!"

"Don't quarrel," said a quiet little voice. "You all put on such horrid, ugly faces when you quarrel, and nobody would ever want you at a party or give you a prize. You are lucky to be big enough and expensive enough to be taken to a party."

It was a small doll who was speaking, with a dear little face, straight hair in two plaits, a soft body and a sweet smile. The curly-haired doll scowled at her.

"How dare you say we have horrid, ugly faces? What about you? Why, your eyes won't even shut, and instead of having a proper body like mine, you're just squashy. Pooh!"

"She's cuddly, anyway," said a toy monkey, joining in. "And all the children love her, even the tiny ones. You think too much of yourselves, you big, expensive toys! Just because you cost a lot of money to buy, and we didn't, you think you can rule the toys and do and say what you like!"

"And who is *this* talking?" cried the big teddy bear, growling again. "A silly little old toy monkey, very dirty and without even a ribbon round his neck! How dare you? Go and get into the empty brick box and be quiet."

"Don't you talk to him like that," said a grey donkey with a straw basket on each side of him to carry goods in. "Monkey's all right. Monkey's kind and jolly. You do nothing but show off and growl. I don't like you—*or* the curly-haired doll—*or* the big golliwog. You're too high and mighty altogether!"

Well, that was too much for the three expensive toys! They chased the toy donkey round and round the room, and the golliwog even found the whip that was used to whip the top, and slashed at the frightened donkey.

He backed into the toy cupboard and got himself wedged between a paintbox and a box of dominoes. The golliwog couldn't whip him then.

The little doll with plaited hair was crying. "You're not to whip the donkey. He's never done you any harm. He's a darling, and he never minds carrying the tiny dolls' house dolls in his baskets, to give them a ride. Leave him alone, you horrid golliwog!"

The little doll was brave. She tried to get the whip from the golliwog but, of course, she couldn't. He pushed her away and she fell down and bumped her head.

Monkey ran to help her up, but the big bear jumped at him and growled. The small doll got up and wiped away her tears.

"Come, Monkey," she said. "We'll go and sit in the toy cupboard with the grey donkey. I'll tell you a story, and we'll be happy."

So Monkey went with the little doll, and left the big toys together. He stuck his head out of the toy-cupboard when he was safely there.

"I did hear that only one prize was going to be given to one family," he called. "So although there are three children belonging to us, and three toys will go to the party—only one of you will win a prize. Ha, ha!"

The three big toys looked at one another. Was that true? They wondered! If three prizes could be won by one family they were sure that each of them would win one. They were so very big, beautiful and expensive! But suppose only *one* prize was given?

The curly-haired doll looked at the magnificent teddy bear. "I think he'd win it," she thought. "He's so very big—and his fur is lovely—and he *has* got a wonderful growl. Even I feel frightened if I hear it! I don't think that black golliwog would win a prize. I think he's very ugly!"

The golliwog looked at the big doll. He thought she was very pretty, and so she was. And that blue frock of hers that went swish-swish when she walked! Her hair was lovely too—just like Jenny's, all silky and curly.

"If only one of us can win a prize, it is sure to be that horrid doll," he thought. "She really *is* very pretty, and she cost more than either I or the bear did. Miss Brown won't know how vain and bad-tempered she is. As for the bear, nobody would give *him* a prize. He's unkind, and he hasn't got a tail, and I hate his big growl!"

The bear was looking at the big black golliwog, with his round, shining eyes and enormous mop of black hair. He thought he was a grand and unusual toy, with his black face and fine coat and trousers.

"He'll be sure to win the prize!" he thought jealously. "I don't know why children like those nasty black golliwogs, but they do. And he's just about the grandest golliwog I ever saw, and I've seen a good many. I wonder now—I just wonder if I could do something to *stop* him winning the prize!"

Well, once a thought like that came into the bear's head he just couldn't stop thinking it again and again. And then he thought of something else!

"I'll wait till he's asleep! I'll get the scissors and I'll cut his coat and his trousers! Nobody would take a golliwog to a party with a torn coat and trousers! Aha! That will teach him not to be so horrid!"

And a strange thought came into the curly-haired doll's head too.

"I know how I can stop the bear from going to the party and winning the prize!" she said to herself. "I can wait till he's asleep, and then I can get the ink-bottle and drip some ink gently all over his head! Nobody would take an inky teddy bear to a party!"

And a bad thought had come into the golliwog's head too. "I believe I know how to stop the curly-haired doll from winning a prize! I'll wait till she's asleep, and then I'll take the scissors and cut off her hair!"

What horrid, unkind thoughts! Oh dear, whoever would have imagined that three lovely, expensive toys like those would be so unkind!

Well, when all the little toys had gone into the toy-cupboard to sleep, and only the three big toys were left outside, quite a lot of things happened!

The golliwog and the curly-haired doll tried to keep awake for a little while, but soon they fell asleep. Only the bear was awake. When he was certain that the golliwog was asleep, he got up, crept to the work-basket, and took out the scissors.

He tiptoed to the golliwog. Snip-snip-snip! He cut the golly's trousers into rags! Snip-snip-snip! He cut the sleeves of his coat and left them in rags too.

Aha! Now the golly wouldn't be taken to the party!

The bear put back the scissors, went back

to his place and fell asleep. Now *he* would win the prize tomorrow!

After a while the curly-haired doll woke up with a jump. "Goodness! I went to sleep after all!" she said. "Now, what had I planned to do? Oh, yes—I was going to pour ink over the bear's head. Is he asleep? Yes, I can hear him snoring."

She went over to the bear. He was certainly very fast asleep. The doll went to Jenny's desk and got a bottle of ink. She tiptoed to the bear again, undid the bottle and tipped it gently over the bear's head.

Drip, drip, drip! Drip, drip, drip! The ink fell down in big black drops, and ran over the bear's head. His ears were

soon black. A little
river of ink ran down
his nose.

He stirred in his
sleep. "It's raining,"
he muttered, sleepily.
"Where's my um-
brella? It's raining."

Then he fell
fast asleep
again, and the
curly-haired

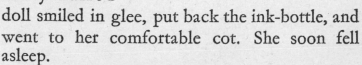

doll smiled in glee, put back the ink-bottle, and
went to her comfortable cot. She soon fell
asleep.

And now it was the golliwog's turn. He
woke up too, and at once remembered what he
had planned to do. Where were the scissors? Ah
—in the basket, of course. He went to fetch
them, and crept over to the doll. He didn't
notice that his coat and trousers were cut and
torn, because it was so dark. There was just
enough light to see the curly-haired doll's head
and face. The golliwog stood behind the doll
and lifted the scissors. Snippity-snip! Snippity-

snip! The doll's curly hair fell in patches on to the pillow.

Ah—now she wouldn't be taken to the party! She looked so queer. The golliwog went to put back the scissors and fell asleep once more.

In the morning, what a to-do! Monkey saw the bear's inky head first and began to giggle.

"Look at the bear! He's all inky! Look at his nose!"

"What's the matter with it?" said the bear, crossly. "My word—look at the curly-haired doll! What's happened to her hair?"

"Oh—look at the golliwog—he's in rags!" cried the doll.

The bear looked at himself in the glass and gave a scream. The curly-haired doll looked at herself, too, and wept big tears to see her head with ragged, short curls instead of the beautiful head of hair she had had.

As for the golliwog, he was furious when he saw his cut clothes. "Who did this? When I find out I'll take the whip that whips the top and give the bad toy such a whipping!" he cried.

All the toys in the toy-cupboard said they

knew nothing about the tricks at all, and goodness knows what would have happened if the
children hadn't come in at that moment.

"We'll just get the curly-haired doll, the
golly and the bear," said Jenny. "And see that
they're nice and tidy for the party."

Thea gave a scream. "Oh! The golliwog's
clothes are cut to ribbons! Look!"

"And LOOK at the curly-haired doll! Her
hair has been cut off," cried Jenny.

"And the bear's head is all black," said Dick,

puzzled. "Can someone have poured ink on him? Good gracious—we can't possibly take any of them with us to the party. They'd never win a prize!"

"Never mind. I'll take the dear little straight-haired doll," said Jenny, picking her up. "She's a darling and I love her because she's cuddly. I'll just replait her hair and wash her face."

"And I'll take Monkey," said Thea. "He's a bit dirty, but I can rub him over with a flannel. I always liked dear old Monkey. He came to bed with me for years each night."

"And I'll take my little grey donkey," said Dick. "He's got such a sweet face. I like him better than the big bear, anyway. The bear always looks so cross."

Well, when they went off to the toys' tea-party, given by Miss Brown, they carried the straight-haired doll, Monkey and the little grey donkey. The curly-haired doll, the golliwog and the bear were left behind.

The doll was crying bitterly. "Who has done these unkind things?" she said, though she knew that she was the one who had poured ink over the bear.

A tiny mouse looked out of a hole in the wall, with his bright eyes twinkling. "*I* know who did them all!" he said. "I peeped last night and saw you! You, curly-haired doll, poured ink over the bear! You, bear, cut the golliwog's clothes. And you, golliwog, cut off the doll's hair. Eee, eee, eee! You all deserved what you got!"

And he turned and shot down his hole at top speed, laughing "eee-eee-eee", all the way.

The toys stared in disgust at the three big

toys. How ashamed they looked! The bear put himself into a corner. The golliwog went and hid behind the coal-scuttle. The curly-haired doll put herself to bed. They didn't say a word, they were so very ashamed.

And what do you think? When the children came home, the straight-haired doll had won first prize! The children ran into the playroom, delighted.

"Little Linda, the straight-haired doll, won the best prize!" cried Jenny. "Everyone said she was the dearest, cuddliest doll they had ever met. So she's got a silver brooch with D for Doll on it. Look—she's wearing it!"

How proud the little doll with plaits felt! Her brooch gleamed on her dress. "I do love it," she said.

"And I did love the tea!" said the monkey. "Real food for us! Fancy that!"

"And real lemonade!" said the grey donkey. "AND I had a bit of real carrot, too. What a party!"

Only three toys didn't want to hear about it. You can guess who they were, can't you?

A Noise in the Night

"I DON'T really see what good you are to our form," said John Benton to Jeff Rayner. "You can't play any game decently, you're such a shrimp—and you're pretty well always at the bottom of the form. You can't even act—and that might have been useful because we've got to do a play this term."

"Well—I can't help being a shrimp, can I?" said Jeff. "I've always been small—and anyway it just happens that this form's got outsize chaps in it. As for being bottom of the form, I can't help that either. I missed two years of school. So shut up about it, John Benton!"

Jeff Rayner looked at John Benton, as he walked away in disgust. He envied him his broad shoulders and sturdy legs. He envied him his place in form. But he knew that he, Jeff, would never do much good at games or lessons.

"I never seem to have caught up, somehow," he thought. "I wish my school-days were over! I wish I didn't have to go to boarding-school, and get ragged at night because I'm such a shrimp. I wish—oh blow, what does it matter what I wish?"

He looked out of the window. "There's a storm blowing up," he thought. "The sky looks angry, and the clouds are simply flying along. Was that thunder?"

"Jeff! There's a talk about animals on the radio—are you coming to hear it?" called a passing boy.

"Right," shouted Jeff, pleased. He never missed a nature talk if he could help it. He knew more about birds and animals than any other boy in the form—not that that was much help to him in lessons or games! He thought of his dog at home—a black cocker spaniel with velvety brown eyes. How he wished the boys were allowed to have their dogs at school! He would certainly have his spaniel, Benny!

"Old Benny doesn't mind if I'm only a shrimp," he thought, going to the common-room where the radio was. "Golly, that *was* thunder! I hope it doesn't thunder and lightning all night long."

The storm drew off after a while, but the sky grew darker and darker. The wind rose and howled round the big school building. By the time it was night there was a howling down the chimneys and a whistling round the windows— to say nothing of mats wriggling about in the draught that blew under every door!

"Going to stand at the window and watch the lightning, John?" asked Jeff, slyly. He knew that John hated storms. It seemed odd to

him that a great, sturdy boy like John, captain of the games and head of form, should always lie cowering in bed at night when a storm came, his sheets pulled high above his head.

"You shut up," said John. "You don't particularly like a storm yourself!"

"No, I don't. But I don't pull my sheets over my head, or tremble so much that my bed shakes!" said Jeff. "There's the thunder again—nearer this time. There *is* going to be a storm."

Jeff was right. No sooner had the boys undressed that night and got into bed than the storm really began. Crash! The thunder rolled round the sky, crashing and rumbling as it went. Then came the rain, pouring down in torrents.

The lightning flashed and lighted up the dormitory. "Well, I never—James and Donald are asleep!" marvelled Jeff. "How *can* they sleep through this?"

But the storm went on so long that even Jeff fell asleep at last, only to be awakened by another crash. He heard John Benton groan in the bed next to his, and he flashed his torch on to him. John had pulled sheets, blanket and rug right over his head!

Then came another crash. Jeff sat up. *That* wasn't thunder, surely? It didn't sound as if it had come from the sky. He listened. The rain came down still, and through the rain he heard another noise.

"That's a dog howling," he thought. "It's frightened. I wonder what's happened."

He sat and listened. The storm died down for a minute, and Jeff could hear the dog again, howling dismally.

"Perhaps it's caught somewhere. I wonder if it's in a trap," thought the boy. "I can't bear the howling. I'll *have* to go and find out."

He shook John. "John—there's a dog howling in pain, somewhere. Come with me and see if we can find him."

"No," said John, from under the clothes. "Good gracious no! You must be mad to think of going out in a storm like this. Don't be an idiot."

Jeff shook the boy in the bed on the other side of him. "Jim—will you come out in the storm with me? There's a dog hurt somewhere."

"Don't be funny," said Jim, and turned over. James and Donald made no stir. They must still

be asleep. There were only five boys in Jeff's dormitory altogether, so there was no one else to wake.

Jeff got out of bed. He felt for his clothes and put them on. He decided to put on his mac downstairs, and find his Wellington boots. He stuffed a torch into his pocket and crept out of the room.

He put on his mac and boots, and borrowed a sou'wester from a peg. He went to the side-door and unbolted it. It made a noise, but the storm was making far more noise!

Jeff stopped on the outside step. What a gale! What torrents of rain! How very very dark!

Then a flash of lightning tore the sky into half, and was followed by a crash of thunder almost overhead.

Jeff hesitated. Everything looked very weird and alarming in that flash of lightning. He didn't at all like stepping out into such a wild night. Then he suddenly thought of something.

The bicycle shed was just opposite. He would get a bike and ride down the drive, out of the gate and down the road. It would be quicker than walking, and if something was waiting to pounce on him as he went by—well, he would be gone before it had him!

So he got out the nearest bicycle, and sailed down the dark drive on it, the lamp making a wavering path of light in front of him.

"Now to find that dog," thought Jeff. "It sounds down this road somewhere. I can still hear it howling. It's either hurt or terribly frightened!"

He cycled on, being almost blown off the
bicycle when he came to the first corner. He got
off to listen. "Yes—the dog's not far off now.
It's one of the farm-dogs, I should think."

He cycled off again down the main road. He
came to a sharp corner and pedalled round. Then
he stopped very abruptly and leapt off—only
just in time! In front of him, stretched across
the road, was something enormous. Something

173

big and dark and sinister-looking. What in the world could it be?

In the feeble light of the bicycle lamp huge black arms stretched up into the air as if they were going to overpower Jeff. The boy was terrified.

Then he suddenly saw what it was.

"It's a tree—an enormous tree blown down across the road by the gale. Goodness, it gave me a fright. That's the noise I heard, I suppose. It woke that dog too, and frightened it. It must be one of the farm-dogs, as I thought. I can hear him whimpering now, but he's safely up at the farm, I'm sure."

The thunder crashed again and made him jump. He was about to mount his bicycle and go back to the school, when a thought struck him.

This main road was used by heavy lorries at night. Dozens of them rumbled along, glad to have a clear road with little traffic for their long journey. Jeff stared at the fallen tree.

"Suppose lorries come along at a good rate, as they always do? They'll swing round this corner and crash into this tree before they even see it! It's only just round the bend of the road."

He stared at the tree again, enormous and bulky, a fallen giant. The rain grew less and stopped. It looked as if the storm was almost over.

"And if it is, the lorries will come along," thought Jeff, in a panic. "They wouldn't be out in that awful storm, they'd be sheltering somewhere—but now they'll all be along again, making up for lost time and going at a good speed. There may be some awful crashes round this corner. But what can I DO?"

He could go back to school, rouse the head and get him to telephone the police. But that would take ages, and by that time there might be some dreadful crashes. If only Jeff had some lamps or road lanterns to set up in front of the tree!

And then an idea flashed into his mind, as quick as a lightning flash.

"I'll tear back to the bicycle shed, and take all the lamps there!" he thought. "I'll pull them from every bicycle—front lamps and back lamps too! And I'll come back and put some on the tree and some at the bend of the road as a warning."

And off he went at top speed, the wind behind him this time, racing swiftly back to the

school gates. In at the gates and up to the bicycle shed—and there Jeff quickly stripped off all the lamps, got a small sack and put them in. He swung it over his shoulder and set off again.

He cycled round the corner and saw the tree once more. Thank goodness no lorry had come along yet! He undid the sack and began to set out the lamps, switching on each one as he did so. Some were red back lamps, some were white front ones.

They made quite a brave show, winking and blinking here and there on the two sides of the fallen tree, for Jeff decided that the other side of the tree should have some too.

He kept back three red ones and placed them at the bend of the road as a warning to lorries to go slow. Then, with no lamps on his bicycle at all, he rode carefully back to school in the dark.

The Headmaster was astonished to hear a knocking at his door a few minutes later. He

opened it and saw a soaking-wet boy in Wellington boots, sou'wester and dripping mac.

"Rayner!" he said, amazed. "Jeff Rayner! What in the world are you doing, dripping wet in the middle of the night?"

"Sir, I heard a noise in the night, and I went to see what it was, and it was a tree blown down across the road at Blind Corner," said Jeff. "You know, sir, lorries come racing along at night, and . . ."

"My word yes! Most dangerous! I must telephone the police at once," said the Head, imagining dozens of lorries suddenly piling up round that dangerous corner. "Go and take those things off. You'd better go to bed too, and get warm. There's nothing you can do, young man—I'll see you in the morning. Good work!"

Jeff was glad to hurry off. He was cold now and shivering, and oddly enough his knees were shaking. Now why should they do that, when all the excitement was over? He stumbled upstairs, suddenly very tired.

He fell into bed, and began to think about all the excitement he had had—but not for long!

His eyes shut firmly, and he was soon dreaming
about bicycle lamps and dogs and trees all mixed
up together.

In the morning he thought it must have been
a dream! John Benton spoke to him. "Well—
did you find the dog?"

"Yes—at least, not exactly," said Jeff. "It
all seems a bit of a muddle now. I found a fallen
tree across the road at Blind Corner, and . . ."

"I bet you didn't!" said John, scornfully. "Buck up—there's the breakfast bell."

The Head did not appear at breakfast, but he came into the Hall as usual to take prayers. With him, most amazingly, was a police Inspector. The boys stared in surprise. Goodness—had somebody done something wrong?

The Head began to speak.

"I think you should all know," he said, "that one of your number heard an unusual noise in the middle of the storm last night, and was brave enough to go out into the storm to find out what it was. He discovered a fallen tree across the road at Blind Corner, where, as you know dozens of lorries swing round every night on their long trips. This boy came back and told me, so that I was able to warn the police and have men sent out there at once."

There was an excited murmuring from the boys. Who had been brave enough to go out on the night of such a storm? "The head-boy, perhaps, the head-boy," the whisper went round.

Then the Inspector took up the tale. "When we got there," he said, "we found the tree festooned with warning lamps, and the corner itself had three lamps as a warning. Would the boy who told the Head about the tree please tell us if he knows who put the lamps there? They must have saved two or three nasty crashes, because some lorries were there before my men got there—and they had all seen the lamps and drawn up in time."

"Jeff Rayner, stand up a moment," said the Head and Jeff, with a face as red as a tomato, stood up. "Do you know who put the lamps

there?" asked the Head. "They appear to have been ordinary bicycle lamps—a most ingenious idea that may have saved many lives."

"Well, sir—yes, I do know, sir," stammered Jeff. "I did, sir! You see, I biked back to the shed and . . ."

But what he was going to say was completely drowned in a roar from all the boys! There was a sudden shouting and cheering and stamping—and even the Head began to clap.

"JEFF! JEFF RAYNER! GOOD OLD JEFF! HURRAH FOR JEFF!" So the shouting went on, almost deafening the surprised Jeff.

Jeff sat down very suddenly, his heart beating fast. Why—the boys were cheering *him*! They weren't laughing at him, sneering, or teasing as they so often did—they were hurrahing and clapping.

"And yet I only did what *they* could have done!" thought Jeff. Ah yes, Jeff—the thing was—they could have done it, but they didn't.

"We'll give a party for Jeff," the boys decided. "He's quite a hero. We'll buy in cakes and all sorts of stuff, and he can sit at the head of the table. Good old Jeff!"

And so that evening, there was a party—and over Jeff's place was a big placard.

HURRAH FOR OUR SHRIMP!
GOOD OLD JEFF!

And now Jeff doesn't in the least mind being called a shrimp. He just grins. His broadest grin was when he had a present from three lorry-drivers—a miniature lorry. It's his most precious possession—and I'm not surprised!